You Can Be a Good Sport, Pout-Pout Fish!

Deborah Diesen

Pictures by Isidre Monés, based on illustrations
created by Dan Hanna for the *New York Times*–
bestselling Pout-Pout Fish books

Farrar Straus Giroux
New York

Farrar Straus Giroux Books for Young Readers
An imprint of Macmillan Publishing Group, LLC
120 Broadway, New York, NY 10271 • mackids.com

Text copyright © 2023 by Deborah Diesen
Pictures copyright © 2023 by Farrar Straus Giroux Books for Young Readers
All rights reserved
Color separations by Embassy Graphics
Printed in China by RR Donnelley Asia Printing Solutions Ltd.,
Dongguan City, Guangdong Province

Designed by Aram Kim and Gene Vosough
First edition, 2023

ISBN: 978-0-374-39106-5 (hardcover)
1 3 5 7 9 10 8 6 4 2

ISBN: 978-0-374-39105-8 (paperback)
1 3 5 7 9 10 8 6 4 2

Library of Congress Cataloging-in-Publication Data is available.

Our books may be purchased in bulk for promotional, educational, or business use.
Please contact your local bookseller or the Macmillan Corporate and Premium Sales Department
at (800) 221-7945 ext. 5442 or by email at MacmillanSpecialMarkets@macmillan.com.

He was on a team.

His team played a game.

His team did not win.

"We scored less than them," said another fish.

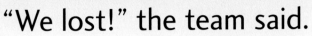

"We lost!" the team said.

Mr. Fish was sad.

The team was sad.

But one fish on the team
was *not* sad.
"That was a great game!"
she said.

"What do you mean?"
asked Mr. Fish. "The other
team won. We lost!"

"But did we try our best?" she asked.

"Yes," said Mr. Fish.

"Did we cheer?" she asked.

"Yes," said Mr. Fish.

"Did we have fun?" she asked.

"Yes," said Mr. Fish.

"Then we won, too," she said.

"We won at being a team!"

The two teams lined up
for high fives.
Mr. Fish and his team said,
"Good game!"

"You, too!" said the other team.

"No pout about it!"